escrito por
Emma Otheguy

ilustrado por
Ana Ramírez González

traducción de
Alexis Romay

UN TRINEO PARA
GABO

A
atheneum

Atheneum Books for Young Readers • Nueva York Londres Toronto Sídney Nueva Delhi

El día de la nevada,
Gabo siguió el sonido
de la vieja calefacción
que silbaba en la cocina.

Se puso en puntillas de pie
y le echó un vistazo a una lata de metal
que subía y bajaba y flotaba en el agua.

"Qué rico", pensó Gabo
antes de que mami viniese
a decirle que se fuera.

Gabo pegó su cara contra la ventana
y su aliento cálido formó una nube de niebla
en el cristal.

La limpió y vio
a unos niños de su nueva escuela
que arrastraban unos trineos a lo alto de la colina
y luego se deslizaban,
dando tumbos y gritos a la par.

Gabo no tenía trineo.

Sus medias eran de algodón, no de lana.

No tenía botas resistentes al agua.

Tenía un gorro con un pompón,
pero le quedaba demasiado pequeño.

—Vamos a resolver —dijo mami.
Ya inventarían algo.

Una media, dos medias, tres medias, cuatro.
Los pies de Gabo estaban calentitos.
Como el gorro de papi le caía por encima de los ojos,
Gabo se enrolló la visera.

Las bolsas de plástico son
resistentes al agua,
así que mami se las amarró
a los tenis de Gabo.

Mami abrió la puerta
y miraron a las casas,
todas en fila.
Contra el cielo grisáceo,
los colores sobresalían.

—Tal vez debería irme a buscar un trineo —dijo Gabo y, con un empujoncito de mami, eso fue lo que hizo.

¡RINNN! ¡RINNN!
¡GUAU! ¡GUAU!

Sancho, el perro del señor
Ramos, ladró alegremente
al ver a Gabo en la puerta.

—Señor Ramos —dijo Gabo—, ¿usted tiene un trineo?

—No tengo trineo —dijo el señor Ramos—.
Pero estoy preparando una tostada de
mermelada de guayaba para Isa,
mi nieta, que viene de visita.
Isa tiene tu edad. ¿Por qué no te quedas un rato?

—No, gracias —dijo Gabo,
que era demasiado tímido
para alguien de su edad.

Afuera, Gabo jugó con Misifú,
un gato que vivía en la tapa
de una alcantarilla y que no era de nadie
y era de todos a la vez.

Misifú hinchó su pecho
y Gabo hizo lo mismo.

Misifú se sacudió el pelaje
y Gabo hizo lo mismo…
esparciendo nieve helada por todas partes.

—¡Gabo, mi amor!

—Hola, señora Tobón —dijo Gabo.

—¿Qué haces con Misifú,
en lugar de estar jugando en la colina?

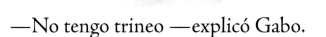

—No tengo trineo —explicó Gabo.

La señora Tobón sacudió la cabeza.
—No te hace falta un trineo para jugar.
¡Mira! Mi mango está maduro y listo
para compartir.

Le ofreció el mango, cuidadosamente
cortado en cubitos,
y señaló con la cabeza hacia la pendiente nevada
en la que los niños patinaban, se deslizaban
y bajaban la colina dando tumbos.

Gabo se metió la mano en el bolsillo
y palpó las sobras del turrón de Navidad.
Había dos crujientes golosinas:
una podría ser para Gabo
y la otra para una nueva amiga,
pero Gabo era demasiado tímido
como para ponerse a repartir cubitos de mango
y sobras del turrón de Navidad.

Gabo arrastró los pies.
Las bolsas de plástico comenzaron
a resbalarse. La nieve se estaba
poniendo gris por todo el tráfico
en el pueblo.

Una señora en la distancia
lo saludó con un guante amarillo en la mano.

—¡Tío Tim! —gritó Gabo—. ¡Madrina!

Tío Tim levantó a Gabo por los aires.
Casi rozó el cielo.

¿Y qué era eso?
Detrás de la espalda de madrina
había un…

—Oh —dijo Gabo,
sintiéndose
empequeñecido
y muy triste.

La bandeja de plástico
era de la cafetería escolar
en la que trabajaba su madrina.

Tenía un lacito amarrado.
Pero la bandeja de plástico
no era un trineo.

¡GUAU! ¡GUAU!

—¡Sancho! —gritó una niña
que tenía que ser Isa,
la nieta del señor Ramos.

Sancho salió dando brincos hacia Gabo
y saltó a sus brazos.

Sancho estaba perfectamente feliz
y a Gabo se le olvidó ser tímido.

—¿Me podrías prestar tu trineo un momento? —preguntó Isa.

—Yo no tengo trineo —dijo Gabo con tristeza.

—¡Claro que tienes un trineo!

—Y, sobre la bandeja de plástico,
Isa se tiró en picado por la pendiente
hasta el pie de la colina.

Subió hasta la cima a la carrera
y, en esa misma bandeja…

Gabo rodó cuesta abajo
dando tumbos y gritos a la par.

Cuando el día de nieve
se volvió un crepúsculo cubierto de hielo
y la colina de los trineos estaba vacía,
la vieja calefacción silbaba
    y la lata de metal
        se enfriaba sobre el mostrador.

Gabo repartió cucharas
y papi le dio varias vueltas
al abrelatas.

—¡DULCE DE LECHE!

—gritaron Gabo e Isa
a la misma vez
y luego metieron las cucharas en la lata.

Gabo se pasó la lengua por los labios
y se metió la mano en el bolsillo
en el que había una golosina más
que *no* le dio timidez compartir.

Para el verdadero Gabo y la verdadera Isa
ahijado querido y sobrinita amada
bilingües y bellos
—E. O.

ATHENEUM BOOKS FOR YOUNG READERS • Un sello editorial de Simon & Schuster Children's Publishing Division • 1230 Avenue of the Americas, New York, New York 10020 • © del texto: 2021, Emma Otheguy • © de las ilustraciones: 2021, Ana Ramírez González • © de la traducción: 2020, Simon & Schuster, Inc. • Traducción de Alexis Romay • Todos los derechos reservados, incluido el derecho de reproducción total o parcial en cualquier formato. • ATHENEUM BOOKS FOR YOUNG READERS es una marca registrada de Simon & Schuster, Inc. El logo de Atheneum es una marca registrada de Simon & Schuster, Inc. • Para obtener información sobre descuentos especiales para compras al por mayor, por favor póngase en contacto con Simon & Schuster Ventas especiales: 1-866-506-1949 o business@simonandschuster.com. • El Simon & Schuster Speakers Bureau puede traer autores a su evento en vivo. Para obtener más información o para reservar a un autor, póngase en contacto con Simon & Schuster Speakers Bureau: 1-866-248-3049 o visite nuestra página web: www.simonspeakers.com. • Diseño del libro: Lauren Rille • El texto de este libro usa las fuentes Jensen. • Hecho en China • 1020 SCP • Primera edición en tapa dura en español, enero 2021 • También disponible en una edición en rústica de Atheneum Books for Young Readers • 10 9 8 7 6 5 4 3 2 1 • Library of Congress Cataloging-in-Publication Data • Names: Otheguy, Emma, author. | Ramírez, Ana, illustrator. | Romay, Alexis, translator. • Title: Un trineo para Gabo / Emma Otheguy ; [ilustrado por Ana Ramirez Gonzalez] ; traducción de Alexis Romay. • Other titles: Sled for Gabo. Spanish • Description: [First edition.] | [New York : Atheneum Books for Young Readers, 2021] | Audience: Ages 4–8. | Audience: Grades 2–3. | Summary: Gabo, shy with other children and having no sled or winter clothing, yearns to go sledding and his neighbor's granddaughter, Isa, helps him find a way. • Identifiers: LCCN 2020026210 | ISBN 9781534445833 (hardcover) | ISBN 9781534495197 (paperback) | ISBN 9781534445857 (eBook) • Subjects: CYAC: Sledding—Fiction. | Bashfulness—Fiction. | Friendship—Fiction. | Hispanic Americans—Fiction. | Spanish language materials. • Classification: LCC PZ73 .O844 2021 | DDC [E]—dc23

Noah,

May God bless you and
keep you all the days of
your life.   Uncle Bill
                &
             Aunt Gracie

ALL ABOUT
JESUS

ALL ABOUT
JESUS

The life and teachings of Jesus
in the Bible's own words

*Selected and illustrated
by Martine Blanc-Rérat*

Loyola Press

Chicago

Published in the U.S.A. by

Loyola Press

3441 North Ashland Avenue
Chicago, Illinois 60657

ISBN 0-8294-1506-8

Designed by
ANDREW MILNE DESIGN

Write to John Hunt Publishing Ltd
46A West Street, Alresford, Hampshire SO24 9AU, UK

Printed in Malaysia

Contents

DEDICATION

To my children and grandchildren:

Marc and Peggy,

Mathurin and Pierre,

Côme, Robin,

and Adrien.

ACKNOWLEDGMENTS

For having consciously or subconsciously helped me realize this book, I would like to thank my parents, children and grandchildren, my sister Marie-Stéphanie, Fatima, my good cousin Marie-Claude, Odile and all my relatives, Father André Van der Borght, Cardinal Jean-Marie Lustiger, Father Antoine Baron, Bishop Jacques Perrier, Father Yves Rozzo, E.N.D's friends, Pascale Bacot, Blandine and Pascal Bourgues, John Hunt.

My very special thanks go to Father Jean-Pascal Duloisy, who has encouraged and advised me with great patience throughout the making of this book; to Marthe Robin, and last, and above all, to my husband, Francis.

Martine Blanc-Rérat

PART ONE

JESUS HAS COME AMONG US

THE CREATION

GENESIS 1:1, 9-11, 24, 27, 28, 31

In the beginning God created the heavens and the earth. And God said, "Let the waters beneath the sky be gathered into one place so dry ground may appear." And so it was. God named the dry ground "land" and the water "seas." And God saw that it was good.

Then God said, "Let the land burst forth with every sort of grass and seed-bearing plant. . . . Let the earth bring forth every kind of animal – livestock, small animals, and wildlife." And so it was.

God created people in his own image; God patterned them after himself; male and female he created them. God blessed them and told them, "Multiply and fill the earth and subdue it. Be masters over the fish and birds and all the animals."

God looked over all he had made, and he saw that it was excellent in every way.

ADAM AND EVE IN THE GARDEN

GENESIS 2:8, 9, 15-17

Then the Lord God planted a garden in Eden, in the east, and there he placed the man he had created. And the Lord God planted all sorts of trees in the garden – beautiful trees that produced delicious fruit. At the center of the garden he placed the tree of life and the tree of the knowledge of good and evil.

The Lord God placed the man in the Garden of Eden to tend and care for it. But the Lord God gave him this warning: "You may freely eat any fruit in the garden except fruit from the tree of the knowledge of good and evil. If you eat of its fruit, you will surely die."

ADAM AND EVE DISOBEY GOD

GENESIS 3:1, 4-6, 5, 17, 22, 23

Now the serpent was the shrewdest of all the creatures the Lord God had made. "You won't die!" the serpent hissed, "God knows that your eyes will be opened when you eat it. You will become just like God, knowing everything, both good and evil."

And to Adam God said, "Because you listened to your wife and ate the fruit I told you not to eat, I have placed a curse on the ground. All your life you will struggle to scratch a living from it."

Then the Lord God said, "What if they eat the fruit of the tree of life? Then they will live forever!" So the Lord God banished Adam and his wife from the Garden of Eden.

GOD SENDS THE FLOOD

GENESIS 6:1, 5, 9, 14, 17, 19; 7:23

Then the human population began to grow rapidly on the earth. Now the Lord observed the extent of the people's wickedness, and he saw that all their thoughts were consistently and totally evil. Noah was the only blameless man living on earth at the time.

God said to Noah, "Make a boat from resinous wood and seal it with tar, inside and out. Look! I am about to cover the earth with a flood. Bring a pair of every kind of animal – a male and a female – into the boat with you to keep them alive during the flood."

Every living thing on the earth was wiped out. Only Noah was left alive, along with those who were with him in the boat.

GOD GIVES THE SIGN OF THE RAINBOW

GENESIS 8:1, 4, 18, 19; 9:8, 11, 13

God sent a wind to blow across the waters, and the floods began to disappear. The boat came to rest on the mountains of Ararat. So Noah, his wife, and his sons and their wives left the boat. And all the various kinds of animals and birds came out, pair by pair.

Then God told Noah and his sons, "I solemnly promise never to send another flood to kill all living creatures and destroy the earth. I have placed my rainbow in the clouds. It is the sign of my permanent promise to you and to all the earth."

GOD CHOOSES A PEOPLE (1850 BC)

GENESIS 12:1, 4, 5; 17:3, 4, 8

Then the Lord told Abram, "Leave your country, your relatives, and your father's house, and go to the land that I will show you."

So Abram departed as the Lord had instructed him. He took his wife, Sarai, his nephew Lot, and all his wealth – his livestock and all the people who had joined his household at Haran – and finally arrived in Canaan.

Then God said to him, "I will make you the father of not just one nation, but a multitude of nations! Yes, I will give all this land of Canaan to you and to your offspring forever. And I will be their God."

GOD GIVES THE TEN COMMANDMENTS (1250 BC)

EXODUS 19:1, 2; 34:28, 29

The Israelites arrived in the wilderness of Sinai exactly two months after they left Egypt. They came to the base of Mount Sinai and set up camp there. Moses was up on the mountain with the Lord forty days and forty nights. At that time he wrote the terms of the covenant – the Ten Commandments – on the stone tablets. When Moses came down the mountain carrying the stone tablets inscribed with the terms of the covenant, he wasn't aware that his face glowed because he had spoken to the Lord face to face.

DAVID'S KINGDOM WILL NEVER END (1000 BC)

2 SAMUEL 7:4, 5, 12, 16, 17

But that same night the Lord said to Nathan, "Go and tell my servant David, 'this is what the Lord says: When you die, I will raise up one of your descendants, and I will make his kingdom strong. Your dynasty and your kingdom will continue for all time before me, and your throne will be secure forever.'"

So Nathan went back to David and told him everything the Lord had said.

THE PROPHET ISAIAH PREDICTS
THE COMING OF JESUS (740 BC)

ISAIAH 7:14; 11:1-2

"All right then, the Lord himself will choose the sign. Look! The virgin will conceive a child! She will give birth to a son and will call him Immanuel – 'God is with us.'

"Out of the stump of David's family will grow a shoot – yes, a new Branch bearing fruit from the old root. And the Spirit of the Lord will rest on him – the Spirit of wisdom and understanding, the Spirit of counsel and might, the Spirit of knowledge and the fear of the Lord."

JESUS' COUNTRY

JESUS IS ANNOUNCED TO MARY

LUKE 1:26-28, 31, 35, 38

God sent the angel Gabriel to Nazareth, a village in Galilee, to a virgin named Mary. She was engaged to be married to a man named Joseph, a descendant of King David.

Gabriel appeared to her and said, "Greetings, favored woman! The Lord is with you! You will become pregnant and have a son, and you are to name him Jesus."

THE BIRTH OF JESUS

LUKE 2:1, 3-7

At that time the Roman emperor, Augustus, decreed that a census should be taken throughout the Roman Empire. All returned to their own towns to register for this census.

And because Joseph was a descendant of King David, he had to go to Bethlehem in Judea, David's ancient home. He traveled there from the village of Nazareth in Galilee. He took with him Mary, his fiancée, who was obviously pregnant by this time.

And while they were there, the time came for her baby to be born. She gave birth to her first child, a son. She wrapped him snugly in strips of cloth and laid him in a manger, because there was no room for them in the village inn.

THE SHEPHERDS HEAR ABOUT JESUS

LUKE 2:8-14

That night some shepherds were in the fields outside the village, guarding their flocks of sheep. Suddenly, an angel of the Lord appeared among them, and the radiance of the Lord's glory surrounded them. They were terribly frightened.

LUKE 2:10-14

But the angel reassured them. "Don't be afraid!" he said. "I bring you good news of great joy for everyone! The Savior – yes, the Messiah, the Lord – has been born tonight in Bethlehem, the city of David! And this is how you will recognize him: You will find a baby lying in a manger, wrapped snugly in strips of cloth!"

Suddenly, the angel was joined by a vast host of others – the armies of heaven – praising God: "Glory to God in the highest heaven, and peace on earth to all whom God favors."

THE SHEPHERDS VISIT JESUS

LUKE 2:15-20

When the angels had returned to heaven, the shepherds said to each other, "Come on, let's go to Bethlehem! Let's see this wonderful thing that has happened, which the Lord has told us about."

They ran to the village and found Mary and Joseph. And there was the baby, lying in the manger.

Then the shepherds told everyone what had happened and what the angel had said to them about this child. All who heard the shepherds' story were astonished.

LUKE 2:19-20

But Mary quietly treasured these things in her heart and thought about them often. The shepherds went back to their fields and flocks, glorifying and praising God for what the angels had told them, and because they had seen the child, just as the angel had said.

THE WISE MEN VISIT JESUS

MATTHEW 2:1-11

Jesus was born in the town of Bethlehem in Judea. About that time some wise men from eastern lands arrived in Jerusalem, asking, "Where is the newborn king of the Jews? We have seen his star as it arose, and we have come to worship him."

MATTHEW 2:9-10

Once again the star appeared to them, guiding them to Bethlehem. It went ahead of them and stopped over the place where the child was.

When they saw the star, they were filled with joy!

They entered the house where the child and his mother, Mary, were, and they fell down before him and worshiped him. Then they opened their treasure chests and gave him gifts of gold, frankincense, and myrrh.

JESUS IS TWELVE YEARS OLD

LUKE 2:41-52

Every year Jesus' parents went to Jerusalem for the Passover festival. When Jesus was twelve years old, they attended the festival as usual. After the celebration was over, they started home to Nazareth, but Jesus stayed behind in Jerusalem. His parents didn't miss him at first, because they assumed he was with friends among the other travelers.

But when he didn't show up that evening, they started to look for him among their relatives and friends. When they couldn't find him, they went back to Jerusalem to search for him there.

Three days later they finally discovered him. He was in the Temple, sitting among the religious teachers, discussing deep questions with them. And all who heard him were amazed at his understanding and his answers.

His parents didn't know what to think.

"Son!" his mother said to him. "Why have you done this to us? Your father and I have been frantic, searching for you everywhere."

"But why did you need to search?" he asked. "You should have known that I would be in my Father's house."

But they didn't understand what he meant.

Then he returned to Nazareth with them and was obedient to them; and his mother stored all these things in her heart.

So Jesus grew both in height and in wisdom, and he was loved by God and by all who knew him.

JOHN THE BAPTIST TELLS THE CROWDS ABOUT JESUS

MARK 1:4, 6-8

This messenger was John the Baptist. He lived in the wilderness and was preaching that people should be baptized to show that they had turned from their sins and turned to God to be forgiven.

His clothes were woven from camel hair, and he wore a leather belt; his food was locusts and wild honey.

He announced: "Someone is coming soon who is far greater than I am – so much greater that I am not even worthy to be his slave. I baptize you with water, but he will baptize you with the Holy Spirit!"

JESUS IS BAPTIZED

MARK 1:9-11

One day Jesus came from Nazareth in Galilee, and he was baptized by John in the Jordan River.

And when Jesus came up out of the water, he saw the heavens split open and the Holy Spirit descending like a dove on him.

And a voice came from heaven saying, "You are my beloved Son, and I am fully pleased with you."

JESUS IN THE DESERT

MATTHEW 4:1-11

Then Jesus was led out into the wilderness by the Holy Spirit to be tempted there by the Devil. For forty days and forty nights he ate nothing and became very hungry.

Then the Devil came and said to him, "If you are the Son of God, change these stones into loaves of bread."

But Jesus told him, "No! The Scriptures say, 'People need more than bread for their life; they must feed on every word of God.'" (*DEUTERONOMY 8:3*)

Then the Devil took him to Jerusalem, to the highest point of the Temple, and said, "If you are the Son of God, jump off! For the Scriptures say,
    'He orders his angels to protect you.
    And they will hold you with their hands to keep you from striking your foot on a stone.'" (*Psalm 91:11-12*)
    Jesus responded, "The Scriptures also say,
    'Do not test the Lord your God.'" (*Deuteronomy 6:16*)

Next the Devil took him to the peak of a very high mountain and showed him the nations of the world and all their glory. "I will give it all to you," he said, "if you will only kneel down and worship me."

"Get out of here, Satan," Jesus told him. "For the Scriptures say,
'You must worship the Lord your God; serve only him.'" (DEUTERONOMY 6:13)
Then the Devil went away, and angels came and cared for Jesus.

JESUS BEGINS TO TEACH

LUKE 4:14-15, 32

Then Jesus returned to Galilee, filled with the Holy Spirit's power. Soon he became well known throughout the surrounding country. He taught in their synagogues and was praised by everyone.

The people were amazed at the things he said, because he spoke with authority.

JESUS HEALS SICK PEOPLE

LUKE 4:40

As the sun went down that evening, people throughout the village brought sick family members to Jesus. No matter what their diseases were, the touch of his hand healed every one.

JESUS CHOOSES HIS FIRST FOLLOWERS

LUKE 5:1-11

One day as Jesus was preaching on the shore of the Sea of Galilee, great crowds pressed in on him to listen to the word of God.

He noticed two empty boats at the water's edge, for the fishermen had left them and were washing their nets.

Stepping into one of the boats, Jesus asked Simon, its owner, to push it out into the water. So he sat in the boat and taught the crowds from there.

When he had finished speaking, he said to Simon, "Now go out where it is deeper and let down your nets, and you will catch many fish."

"Master," Simon replied, "we worked hard all last night and didn't catch a thing. But if you say so, we'll try again."

And this time their nets were so full they began to tear!

A shout for help brought their partners in the other boat, and soon both boats were filled with fish and on the verge of sinking.

When Simon Peter realized what had happened, he fell to his knees before Jesus and said, "Oh, Lord, please leave me – I'm too much of a sinner to be around you."

For he was awestruck by the size of their catch, as were the others with him.

His partners, James and John, the sons of Zebedee, were also amazed.

Jesus replied to Simon, "Don't be afraid! From now on you'll be fishing for people!"

And as soon as they landed, they left everything and followed Jesus.

PART TWO

JESUS HAS COME TO SAVE THOSE WHO ARE LOST

JESUS HEALS A MAN
WITH A SKIN DISEASE

MATTHEW 8:1-3

Large crowds followed Jesus as he came down the mountainside. Suddenly, a man with leprosy approached Jesus. He knelt before him, worshiping. "Lord," the man said, "if you want to, you can make me well again."

Jesus touched him. "I want to," he said. "Be healed!"

And instantly the leprosy disappeared.

JESUS HEALS SIMON'S MOTHER-IN-LAW

MARK 1:29-31

After Jesus and his disciples left the synagogue, they went over to Simon and Andrew's home, and James and John were with them.

Simon's mother-in-law was sick in bed with a high fever. They told Jesus about her right away.

He went to her bedside, and as he took her by the hand and helped her to sit up, the fever suddenly left, and she got up and prepared a meal for them.

JESUS HEALS AND FORGIVES

MARK 2:1-12

Several days later Jesus returned to Capernaum, and the news of his arrival spread quickly through the town. Soon the house where he was staying was so packed with visitors that there wasn't room for one more person, not even outside the door. And he preached the word to them.

Four men arrived carrying a paralyzed man on a mat.

They couldn't get to Jesus through the crowd, so they dug through the clay roof above his head. Then they lowered the sick man on his mat, right down in front of Jesus.

Seeing their faith, Jesus said to the paralyzed man, "My son, your sins are forgiven."

But some of the teachers of religious law who were sitting there said to themselves, "What? This is blasphemy! Who but God can forgive sins!"

Jesus knew what they were discussing among themselves, so he said to them, "Why do you think this is blasphemy? Is it easier to say to the paralyzed man, 'Your sins are forgiven' or 'Get up, pick up your mat, and walk'?

"I will prove that I, the Son of Man, have the authority on earth to forgive sins."

Then Jesus turned to the paralyzed man and said, "Stand up, take your mat, and go on home, because you are healed!"

The man jumped up, took the mat, . . .

. . . and pushed his way through the stunned onlookers.

Then they all praised God. "We've never seen anything like this before!" they exclaimed.

JESUS CALLS SINNERS TO CHANGE THEIR LIVES

LUKE 5:27-32

Later, as Jesus left the town, he saw a tax collector named Levi sitting at his tax-collection booth. "Come, be my disciple!" Jesus said to him.

So Levi got up, left everything, and followed him.

Soon Levi held a banquet in his home with Jesus as the guest of honor. Many of Levi's fellow tax collectors and other guests were there. But the Pharisees and their teachers of religious law complained bitterly to Jesus' disciples, "Why do you eat and drink with such scum?"

Jesus answered them, "Healthy people don't need a doctor – sick people do.
"I have come to call sinners to turn from their sins, not to spend my time with those who think they are already good enough."

JESUS HEALS A WOMAN AND A GIRL

MARK 5:21-43

When Jesus went back across to the other side of the lake, a large crowd gathered around him on the shore. A leader of the local synagogue, whose name was Jairus, came and fell down before him, pleading with him to heal his little daughter.

"She is about to die," he said in desperation. "Please come and place your hands on her; heal her so she can live."

Jesus went with him, and the crowd thronged behind.

And there was a woman in the crowd who had had a hemorrhage for twelve years. She had suffered a great deal from many doctors through the years and had spent everything she had to pay them, but she had gotten no better. In fact, she was worse.

She had heard about Jesus, so she came up behind him through the crowd and touched the fringe of his robe. For she thought to herself, "If I can just touch his clothing, I will be healed."

Immediately the bleeding stopped, and she could feel that she had been healed!

Jesus realized at once that healing power had gone out from him, so he turned around in the crowd and asked, "Who touched my clothes?"

His disciples said to him, "All this crowd is pressing around you. How can you ask, 'Who touched me?'"

But he kept on looking around to see who had done it.

Then the frightened woman, trembling at the realization of what had happened to her, came and fell at his feet and told him what she had done.

And he said to her, "Daughter, your faith has made you well. Go in peace. You have been healed."

While he was still speaking to her, messengers arrived from Jairus's home with the message, "Your daughter is dead. There's no use troubling the Teacher now."

But Jesus ignored their comments and said to Jairus, "Don't be afraid. Just trust me."

Then Jesus stopped the crowd and wouldn't let anyone go with him except Peter and James and John.

When they came to the home of the synagogue leader, Jesus saw the commotion and the weeping and wailing. He went inside and spoke to the people. "Why all this weeping and commotion?" he asked. "The child isn't dead; she is only asleep."

The crowd laughed at him, but he told them all to go outside. Then he took the girl's father and mother and his three disciples into the room where the girl was lying.

Holding her hand, he said to her, "Get up, little girl!" And the girl, who was twelve years old, immediately stood up and walked around! Her parents were absolutely overwhelmed.

Jesus commanded them not to tell anyone what had happened, and he told them to give her something to eat.

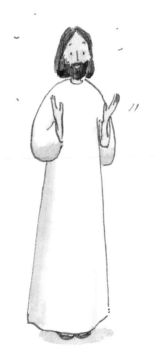

THE STORY OF THE LOST SHEEP

LUKE 15:3-7

So Jesus used this illustration: "If you had one hundred sheep, and one of them strayed away and was lost in the wilderness, . . .

". . . wouldn't you leave the ninety-nine others to go and search for the lost one . . .

". . . until you found it?

"And then you would joyfully carry it home on
your shoulders.

"When you arrived, you would call together your friends and neighbors to rejoice with you because your lost sheep was found.

"In the same way, heaven will be happier over one lost sinner who returns to God than over ninety-nine others who are righteous and haven't strayed away!"

THE STORY OF THE LOST SON

LUKE 15:11-32

To illustrate the point further, Jesus told them this story: "A man had two sons.

"The younger son told his father, 'I want my share of your estate now, instead of waiting until you die.' So his father agreed to divide his wealth between his sons.

"A few days later this younger son
packed all his belongings and took a trip to
a distant land, . . .

". . . and there he wasted all his money on wild living.

"About the time his money ran out, a great famine swept over the land, and he began to starve.

"He persuaded a local farmer to hire him to feed his pigs.

"The boy became so hungry that even the pods he was feeding the pigs looked good to him. But no one gave him anything.

"When he finally came to his senses, he said to himself, 'At home even the hired men have food enough to spare, and here I am, dying of hunger! I will go home to my father and say, "Father, I have sinned against both heaven and you, and I am no longer worthy of being called your son. Please take me on as a hired man."'

"So he returned home to his father.

"And while he was still a long distance away, his father saw him coming. Filled with love and compassion, . . .

" . . . he ran to his son, embraced him, . . .

". . . and kissed him.

"His son said to him, 'Father, I have sinned against both heaven and you, and I am no longer worthy of being called your son.'

"But his father said to the servants, 'Quick! Bring the finest robe in the house and put it on him.

"'Get a ring for his finger, and sandals for his feet.

"'And kill the calf we have been fattening in the pen. We must celebrate with a feast, for this son of mine was dead and has now returned to life. He was lost, but now he is found.'

"So the party began.

"Meanwhile, the older son was in the fields working. When he returned home, he heard music and dancing in the house, and he asked one of the servants what was going on.

"'Your brother is back,' he was told, 'and your father has killed the calf we were fattening and has prepared a great feast. We are celebrating because of his safe return.'

"The older brother was angry and wouldn't go in.

"His father came out and begged him, but he replied, 'All these years I've worked hard for you and never once refused to do a single thing you told me to. And in all that time you never gave me even one young goat for a feast with my friends. Yet when this son of yours comes back after squandering your money on prostitutes, you celebrate by killing the finest calf we have.'

"His father said to him, 'Look, dear son, you and I are very close, and everything I have is yours. We had to celebrate this happy day. For your brother was dead and has come back to life! He was lost, but now he is found!'"

PART THREE

JESUS SHOWS US
HOW TO LOVE

JESUS CHOOSES HIS TWELVE APOSTLES

LUKE 6:12-16

One day soon afterward Jesus went to a mountain to pray, . . .

. . . and he prayed to God all night.

At daybreak he called together all of his disciples . . .

. . . and chose twelve of them to be apostles. Here are their names: Simon (he also called him Peter), Andrew (Peter's brother), James, John, Philip, Bartholomew, Matthew, Thomas, James (son of Alphaeus), Simon (the Zealot), Judas (son of James), Judas Iscariot (who later betrayed him).

JESUS TEACHES US ABOUT
REAL HAPPINESS

MATTHEW 5:1-12

One day as the crowds were gathering, Jesus went up the mountainside with his disciples and sat down to teach them. This is what he taught them:

"God blesses those who realize their need for him, for the Kingdom of Heaven is given to them.

God blesses those who mourn, for they will be comforted.

God blesses those who are gentle and lowly, for the whole earth will belong to them.

God blesses those who are hungry and thirsty for justice, for they will receive it in full.

God blesses those who are merciful, for they will be shown mercy.

God blesses those whose hearts are pure, for they will see God.

God blesses those who work for peace, for they will be called the children of God.

God blesses those who are persecuted because they live for God, for the Kingdom of Heaven is theirs.

God blesses you when you are mocked and persecuted and lied about because you are my followers. Be happy about it! Be very glad! For a great reward awaits you in heaven. And remember, the ancient prophets were persecuted, too."

JESUS TEACHES US HOW TO LOVE

LUKE 6:27-28, 31, 35, 37, 38

But if you are willing to listen, I say, love your enemies. Do good to those who hate you.

"Pray for the happiness of those who curse you. Pray for those who hurt you.

"Do for others as you would like them to do for you.

"Love your enemies! Do good to them! Lend to them! And don't be concerned that they might not repay.

"Stop judging others, and you will not be judged. Stop criticizing others, or it will all come back on you. If you forgive others, you will be forgiven. If you give, you will receive."

JESUS TELLS US HOW TO FORGIVE

MATTHEW 18:21-22

Then Peter came to him and asked, "Lord, how often should I forgive someone who sins against me? Seven times?"

"No!" Jesus replied, "seventy times seven!"

THE STORY OF THE GOOD SAMARITAN

LUKE 10:25-37

One day an expert in religious law stood up to test Jesus by asking him this question: "Teacher, what must I do to receive eternal life?"

Jesus replied, "What does the law of Moses say? How do you read it?"

The man answered, "'You must love the Lord your God with all your heart, all your soul, all your strength, and all your mind.' And, 'Love your neighbor as yourself.'"

"Right!" Jesus told him. "Do this and you will live!"

The man wanted to justify his actions, so he asked Jesus, "And who is my neighbor?"

Jesus replied with an illustration: "A Jewish man was traveling on a trip from Jerusalem to Jericho, . . .

".. . and he was attacked by bandits. They stripped him of his clothes and money, beat him up, . . .

". . . and left him half dead beside the road.

"By chance a Jewish priest came along; but when he saw the man lying there, he crossed to the other side of the road and passed him by.

"A Temple assistant walked over and looked at him lying there, but he also passed by on the other side.

"Then a despised
Samaritan came along,
and when he saw the
man, he felt deep pity.

"Kneeling beside him,
the Samaritan soothed
his wounds with
medicine and bandaged
them.

"Then he put the man on his own donkey and took him to an inn, where he took care of him.

"The next day he handed the innkeeper two pieces of silver and told him to take care of the man.

"'If his bill runs higher than that,' he said, 'I'll pay the difference the next time I am here.'

"Now which of these three would you say was a neighbor to the man who was attacked by bandits?" Jesus asked.

The man replied, "The one who showed him mercy."

Then Jesus said, "Yes, now go and do the same."

JESUS TEACHES US TO PRAY

MATTHEW 6:9-13

Jesus said to his followers:
"Pray like this: Our Father in heaven, may your name be honored.
May your Kingdom come soon.
May your will be done here on earth, just as it is in heaven.
Give us our food for today, and forgive us our sins, just as we have forgiven those who have sinned against us.
And don't let us yield to temptation, but deliver us from the evil one."

MARK 11:25

"But when you are praying, first forgive anyone you are holding a grudge against, so that your Father in heaven will forgive your sins, too."

JESUS TEACHES US ABOUT
REAL TREASURE

MATTHEW 6:19-21

Jesus said to his followers:
"Don't store up treasures here on earth, . . .

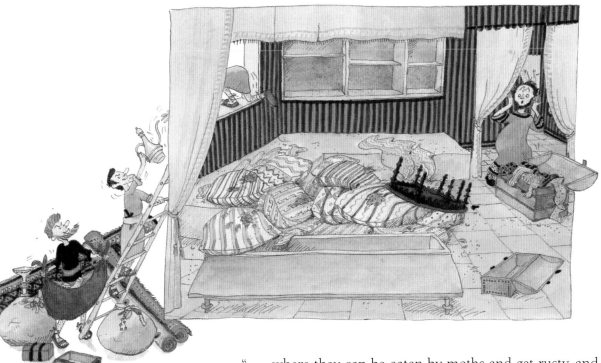

"... where they can be eaten by moths and get rusty, and where thieves break in and steal. Store your treasures in heaven, where they will never become moth-eaten or rusty and where they will be safe from thieves. Wherever your treasure is, there your heart and thoughts will also be."

JESUS TELLS US NOT TO WORRY

MATTHEW 6:24-26, 28-29, 31-33

Jesus said to his followers: "You cannot serve both God and money.
"So I tell you, don't worry about everyday life – whether you have enough food, drink, and clothes. Doesn't life consist of more than food and clothing?
"Look at the birds. They don't need to plant or harvest or put food in barns because your heavenly Father feeds them. And you are far more valuable to him than they are.

"And why worry about your clothes? Look at the lilies and how they grow. They don't work or make their clothing, yet Solomon in all his glory was not dressed as beautifully as they are.

"So don't worry about having enough food or drink or clothing. Why be like the pagans who are so deeply concerned about these things? Your heavenly Father already knows all your needs, and he will give you all you need from day to day if you live for him and make the Kingdom of God your primary concern."

123

THE STORY OF THE PHARISEE AND
THE TAX COLLECTOR

LUKE 18:9-14

Then Jesus told this story to some who had great self-confidence and scorned everyone else:

"Two men went to the Temple to pray. One was a Pharisee, and the other was a dishonest tax collector.

"The proud Pharisee stood by himself and prayed this prayer: 'I thank you, God, that I am not a sinner like everyone else, especially like that tax collector over there! For I never cheat, I don't sin, I don't commit adultery, I fast twice a week, and I give you a tenth of my income.'

"But the tax collector stood at a distance and dared not even lift his eyes to heaven as he prayed. Instead, he beat his chest in sorrow, saying, 'O God, be merciful to me, for I am a sinner.' I tell you, this sinner, not the Pharisee, returned home justified before God. For the proud will be humbled, but the humble will be honored."

JESUS AND THE SMALL CHILDREN

MARK 10:13-16

One day some parents brought their children to Jesus so he could touch them and bless them, but the disciples told them not to bother him.

But when Jesus saw what was happening, he was very displeased with his disciples. He said to them, "Let the children come to me. Don't stop them! For the Kingdom of God belongs to such as these.

127

"I assure you, anyone who doesn't have their kind of faith will never get into the Kingdom of God."

Then he took the children into his arms and placed his hands on their heads and blessed them.

WE MUST DO WHAT JESUS TELLS US

LUKE 6:47-49

Jesus said to his followers: "I will show you what it's like when someone comes to me, listens to my teaching, and then obeys me. It is like a person who builds a house on a strong foundation laid upon the underlying rock.

"When the floodwaters rise and break against the house, it stands firm because it is well built.

"But anyone who listens and doesn't obey is like a person who builds a house without a foundation.

"When the floods sweep down against that house, it will crumble into a heap of ruins."

JESUS SENDS HIS TWELVE APOSTLES
ON A MISSION

LUKE 9:1-2, 6

One day Jesus called together his twelve apostles and gave them power and authority to cast out demons and to heal all diseases. Then he sent them out to tell everyone about the coming of the Kingdom of God and to heal the sick.

So they began their circuit of the villages, preaching the Good News and healing the sick.

PART FOUR

WHO IS JESUS?

JESUS STOPS A STORM

MATTHEW 8:23-27

Then Jesus got into the boat and started across the lake with his disciples. Suddenly, a terrible storm came up, with waves breaking into the boat. But Jesus was sleeping. The disciples went to him and woke him up, shouting, "Lord, save us! We're going to drown!"

And Jesus answered, "Why are you afraid? You have so little faith!"

Then he stood up and rebuked the wind and waves, and suddenly all was calm. The disciples just sat there in awe. "Who is this?" they asked themselves. "Even the wind and waves obey him!"

Jesus Has Water for Thirsty People

John 4:4, 6-11, 13-14

Jesus had to go through Samaria.
Jacob's well was there; and Jesus, tired from the long walk, sat wearily beside the well about noontime. Soon a Samaritan woman came to draw water, and Jesus said to her, "Please give me a drink." He was alone at the time because his disciples had gone into the village to buy some food.

The woman was surprised, for Jews refuse to have anything to do with Samaritans. She said to Jesus, "You are a Jew, and I am a Samaritan woman. Why are you asking me for a drink?"

Jesus replied, "If you only knew the gift God has for you and who I am, you would ask me, and I would give you living water."

"But sir, you don't have a rope or a bucket," she said, "and this is a very deep well. Where would you get this living water?"

Jesus replied, "People soon become thirsty again after drinking this water. But the water I give them takes away thirst altogether. It becomes a perpetual spring within them, giving them eternal life."

JESUS FEEDS OVER 5,000 HUNGRY PEOPLE

JOHN 6:3-15

Then Jesus went up into the hills and sat down with his disciples around him. (It was nearly time for the annual Passover celebration.)

Jesus soon saw a great crowd of people climbing the hill, looking for him. Turning to Philip, he asked, "Philip, where can we buy bread to feed all these people?" He was testing Philip, for he already knew what he was going to do.

Philip replied, "It would take a small fortune to feed them!"

Then Andrew, Simon Peter's brother, spoke up. "There's a young boy here with five barley loaves and two fish. But what good is that with this huge crowd?"

"Tell everyone to sit down," Jesus ordered.

So all of them – the men alone numbered five thousand – sat down on the grassy slopes.

Then Jesus took the loaves, gave thanks to God, . . .

. . . and passed them out to the people. Afterward he did the same with the fish. And they all ate until they were full.

"Now gather the leftovers," Jesus told his disciples, "so that nothing is wasted."
There were only five barley loaves to start with, but twelve baskets were filled
with the pieces of bread the people did not eat!

When the people saw this miraculous sign, they exclaimed, "Surely, he is the Prophet we have been expecting!"

Jesus saw that they were ready to take him by force and make him king, so he went higher into the hills alone.

JESUS WILL GIVE HIMSELF AS FOOD

JOHN 6:22, 24-26, 32-35, 51, 55-56

The next morning, back across the lake, crowds began gathering on the shore, waiting to see Jesus. When the crowd saw that Jesus wasn't there, nor his disciples, they got into the boats and went across to Capernaum to look for him.

When they arrived and found him, they asked, "Teacher, how did you get here?"

Jesus replied, "The truth is, you want to be with me because I fed you, not because you saw the miraculous sign."

Jesus said, "My Father . . . now . . . offers you the true bread from heaven. The true bread of God is the one who comes down from heaven and gives life to the world."

"Sir," they said, "give us that bread every day of our lives."

Jesus replied, "I am the bread of life. No one who comes to me will ever be hungry again. Those who believe in me will never thirst.

"This bread is my flesh, offered so the world may live.

"For my flesh is the true food, and my blood is the true drink. All who eat my flesh and drink my blood remain in me, and I in them."

JESUS IS THE GOOD SHEPHERD

JOHN 10:11-15

Jesus said, "I am the good shepherd. The good shepherd lays down his life for the sheep.

"A hired hand will run when he sees a wolf coming. He will leave the sheep because they aren't his and he isn't their shepherd.

147

"And so the wolf attacks them and scatters the flock. The hired hand runs away because he is merely hired and has no real concern for the sheep.

"I am the good shepherd; I know my own sheep, and they know me, just as my Father knows me and I know the Father. And I lay down my life for the sheep."

WHO IS JESUS?

MATTHEW 16:15-16, 20-21

Then he asked his followers, "Who do you say I am?"

Simon Peter answered, "You are the Messiah, the Son of the living God."

Then Jesus sternly warned them not to tell anyone that he was the Messiah.

From then on Jesus began to tell his disciples plainly that he had to go to Jerusalem, and he told them what would happen to him there. He would suffer at the hands of the leaders and the leading priests and the teachers of religious law. He would be killed, and he would be raised on the third day.

HOW TO FOLLOW JESUS

MATTHEW 16:24-26

Then Jesus said to the disciples, "If any of you wants to be my follower, you must put aside your selfish ambition, shoulder your cross, and follow me. If you try to keep your life for yourself, you will lose it. But if you give up your life for me, you will find true life.

"And how do you benefit if you gain the whole world but lose your own soul in the process? Is anything worth more than your soul?"

JESUS WITH MOSES AND ELIJAH

MARK 9:2-10

Six days later Jesus took Peter and the two brothers, James and John, and led them up a high mountain.

As the men watched, Jesus' appearance changed so that his face shone like the sun, and his clothing became dazzling white.

Suddenly, Moses and Elijah appeared and began talking with Jesus.

Peter blurted out, "Lord, this is wonderful! If you want me to, I'll make three shrines, one for you, one for Moses, and one for Elijah."

But even as he said it, a bright cloud came over them, and a voice from the cloud said, "This is my beloved Son, and I am fully pleased with him. Listen to him."

The disciples were terrified and fell face down on the ground.
Jesus came over and touched them. "Get up," he said, "don't be afraid." And when they looked, they saw only Jesus with them.

As they descended the mountain, Jesus commanded them, "Don't tell anyone what you have seen until I, the Son of Man, have been raised from the dead."

JESUS BRINGS LAZARUS BACK TO LIFE

JOHN 11:1, 5-7, 20-22, 32, 38-48, 53-56

A man named Lazarus was sick. He lived in Bethany with his sisters, Mary and Martha.

Although Jesus loved Martha, Mary, and Lazarus, he stayed where he was for the next two days and did not go to them. Finally after two days, he said to his disciples, "Let's go to Judea again."

When Martha got word that Jesus was coming, she went to meet him. But Mary stayed at home.

Martha said to Jesus, "Lord, if you had been here, my brother would not have died. But even now I know that God will give you whatever you ask."

When Mary arrived and saw Jesus, she fell down at his feet and said, "Lord, if you had been here, my brother would not have died."

They came to the grave. It was a cave with a stone rolled across its entrance.

"Roll the stone aside," Jesus told them.

But Martha, the dead man's sister, said, "Lord, by now the smell will be terrible because he has been dead for four days."

Jesus responded, "Didn't I tell you that you will see God's glory if you believe?"

So they rolled the stone aside. Then Jesus looked up to heaven and said, "Father, thank you for hearing me. You always hear me, but I said it out loud for the sake of all these people standing here, so they will believe you sent me."

Then Jesus shouted, "Lazarus, come out!"

And Lazarus came out, bound in graveclothes, his face wrapped in a headcloth.

Jesus told them, "Unwrap him and let him go!"

Many of the people who were with Mary believed in Jesus when they saw this happen.

But some went to the Pharisees and told them what Jesus had done.

Then the leading priests and Pharisees called the high council together to discuss the situation. "What are we going to do?" they asked each other. "This man certainly performs many miraculous signs. If we leave him alone, the whole nation will follow him, and then the Roman army will come and destroy both our Temple and our nation."

So from that time on the Jewish leaders began to plot Jesus' death.

As a result, Jesus stopped his public ministry among the people and left Jerusalem. He went to a place near the wilderness, to the village of Ephraim, and stayed there with his disciples.

It was now almost time for the celebration of Passover, and many people from the country arrived in Jerusalem several days early so they could go through the cleansing ceremony before the Passover began. They wanted to see Jesus, and as they talked in the Temple, they asked each other, "What do you think? Will he come for the Passover?"

PART FIVE

JESUS GIVES HIS LIFE FOR US

JUDAS DECIDES TO BETRAY JESUS

JOHN 11:57; MATTHEW 26:14-16

Meanwhile, the leading priests and Pharisees had publicly announced that anyone seeing Jesus must report him immediately so they could arrest him.

Then Judas Iscariot, one of the twelve disciples, went to the leading priests and asked, "How much will you pay me to betray Jesus to you?"

And they gave him thirty pieces of silver. From that time on, Judas began looking for the right time and place to betray Jesus.

THE CROWDS CHEER JESUS

JOHN 12:12-13, 17

The next day, the news that Jesus was on the way to Jerusalem swept through the city. A huge crowd of Passover visitors took palm branches and went down the road to meet him. They shouted,
"Praise God!
Bless the one who comes in the name of the Lord!
Hail to the King of Israel!" (*PSALM 118:25-26*)
Those in the crowd who had seen Jesus call Lazarus back to life were telling others all about it.

JESUS' LAST MEAL

LUKE 22:7-8, 13-15

Now the Festival of Unleavened Bread arrived, when the Passover lambs were sacrificed.

Jesus sent Peter and John ahead and said, "Go and prepare the Passover meal, so we can eat it together."

They went off . . . and they prepared the Passover supper.

Then at the proper time Jesus and the twelve apostles sat down together at the table. Jesus said, "I have looked forward to this hour with deep longing, anxious to eat this Passover meal with you before my suffering begins."

JESUS BECOMES HIS FOLLOWERS' SERVANT

JOHN 13:4-5, 12, 15

Jesus got up from the table, took off his robe, wrapped a towel around his waist, and poured water into a basin. Then he began to wash the disciples' feet and to wipe them with the towel he had around him.

After washing their feet, he put on his robe again and sat down and asked, "Do you understand what I was doing?

"I have given you an example to follow. Do as I have done to you."

THE FIRST LORD'S SUPPER

MATTHEW 26:26-28

As they were eating, Jesus took a loaf of bread and asked God's blessing on it. Then he broke it in pieces and gave it to the disciples, saying, "Take it and eat it, for this is my body."

And he took a cup of wine and gave thanks to God for it. He gave it to them and said, "Each of you drink from it, for this is my blood, which seals the covenant between God and his people. It is poured out to forgive the sins of many."

JESUS SAYS THAT JUDAS IS GOING TO BETRAY HIM

JOHN 13:21-26, 30

Now Jesus was in great anguish of spirit, and he exclaimed, "The truth is, one of you will betray me!"

The disciples looked at each other, wondering whom he could mean.

One of Jesus' disciples, the one Jesus loved, was sitting next to Jesus at the table. Simon Peter motioned to him to ask who would do this terrible thing. Leaning toward Jesus, he asked, "Lord, who is it?"

Jesus said, "It is the one to whom I give the bread dipped in the sauce." And when he had dipped it, he gave it to Judas, son of Simon Iscariot.

So Judas left at once, going out into the night.

JESUS GIVES A NEW COMMAND

JOHN 13:31, 33, 34-35

As soon as Judas left the room, Jesus said, "The time has come for me, the Son of Man, to enter into my glory, and God will receive glory because of all that happens to me. Dear children, how brief are these moments before I must go away and leave you! So now I give you a new commandment: Love each other. Just as I have loved you, you should love each other. Your love for one another will prove to the world that you are my disciples."

JESUS IS THE WAY TO THE FATHER

JOHN 14:6, 8, 9

Jesus told Thomas, "I am the way, the truth, and the life. No one can come to the Father except through me."

Philip said, "Lord, show us the Father and we will be satisfied."

Jesus replied, "Philip, don't you even yet know who I am, even after all the time I have been with you? Anyone who has seen me has seen the Father! So why are you asking to see him?"

JESUS WILL SEND THE HOLY SPIRIT

JOHN 14:23, 25-26

Jesus replied, "All those who love me will do what I say. My Father will love them, and we will come to them and live with them.

"I am telling you these things now while I am still with you. But when the Father sends the Counselor as my representative – and by the Counselor I mean the Holy Spirit – he will teach you everything and will remind you of everything I myself have told you."

JESUS IS THE VINE; WE ARE THE BRANCHES

JOHN 15:4-5

Jesus said to his followers: "Remain in me, and I will remain in you. For a branch cannot produce fruit if it is severed from the vine, and you cannot be fruitful apart from me.

"Yes, I am the vine; you are the branches. Those who remain in me, and I in them, will produce much fruit. For apart from me you can do nothing."

JESUS WANTS TO SHARE HIS JOY WITH US

JOHN 15:10-11, 14, 17

When you obey me, you remain in my love, just as I obey my Father and remain in his love. I have told you this so that you will be filled with my joy. Yes, your joy will overflow!

"You are my friends if you obey me. I command you to love each other."

THE SUFFERING OF JESUS

LUKE 22:39-44

Then, accompanied by the disciples, Jesus left the upstairs room and went as usual to the Mount of Olives. There he told them, "Pray that you will not be overcome by temptation."

He walked away, about a stone's throw, and knelt down and prayed, "Father, if you are willing, please take this cup of suffering away from me. Yet I want your will, not mine."

Then an angel from heaven appeared and strengthened him. He prayed more fervently, and he was in such agony of spirit that his sweat fell to the ground like great drops of blood.

JESUS IS ARRESTED

LUKE 22:45-48, 52-54, 63-65

At last Jesus stood up again and returned to the disciples, only to find them asleep, exhausted from grief.

"Why are you sleeping?" he asked. "Get up and pray. Otherwise temptation will overpower you."

But even as he said this, a mob approached, led by Judas, one of his twelve disciples.

Judas walked over to Jesus and greeted him with a kiss. But Jesus said, "Judas, how can you betray me, the Son of Man, with a kiss?"

Then Jesus spoke to the leading priests and captains of the Temple guard and the other leaders who headed the mob. "Am I some dangerous criminal," he asked, "that you have come armed with swords and clubs to arrest me? Why didn't you arrest me in the Temple? I was there every day. But this is your moment, the time when the power of darkness reigns."

So they arrested him and led him to the high priest's residence, and Peter was following far behind.

Now the guards in charge of Jesus began mocking and beating him. They blindfolded him; then they hit him and asked, "Who hit you that time, you prophet?"

And they threw all sorts of terrible insults at him.

JESUS BEFORE THE HIGHEST COURT

LUKE 22:66, 70, 71; 23:1

At daybreak all the leaders of the people assembled, including the leading priests and the teachers of religious law. Jesus was led before this high council.

They all shouted, "Then you claim you are the Son of God?"

And he replied, "You are right in saying that I am."

Then the entire council took Jesus over to Pilate, the Roman governor.

JESUS BEFORE PILATE

LUKE 23:4-7

Pilate turned to the leading priests and to the crowd and said, "I find nothing wrong with this man!"

Then they became desperate. "But he is causing riots everywhere he goes, all over Judea, from Galilee to Jerusalem!"

"Oh, is he a Galilean?" Pilate asked. When they answered that he was, Pilate sent him to Herod Antipas, because Galilee was under Herod's jurisdiction, and Herod happened to be in Jerusalem at the time.

JESUS BEFORE HEROD

LUKE 23:8-12

Herod was delighted at the opportunity to see Jesus, because he had heard about him and had been hoping for a long time to see him perform a miracle. He asked Jesus question after question, but Jesus refused to answer. Meanwhile, the leading priests and the teachers of religious law stood there shouting their accusations. Now Herod and his soldiers began mocking and ridiculing Jesus. Then they put a royal robe on him and sent him back to Pilate. Herod and Pilate, who had been enemies before, became friends that day.

JESUS AGAIN BEFORE PILATE

LUKE 23:13, 15-21

Then Pilate called together the leading priests and other religious leaders, along with the people.

Pilate said, "Nothing this man has done calls for the death penalty. So I will have him flogged, but then I will release him."

Then a mighty roar rose from the crowd, and with one voice they shouted, "Kill him, and release Barabbas to us!" (Barabbas was in prison for murder and for taking part in an insurrection in Jerusalem against the government.)

Pilate argued with them, because he wanted to release Jesus. But they shouted, "Crucify him! Crucify him!"

JOHN 19:1-3

Then Pilate had Jesus flogged with a lead-tipped whip. The soldiers made a crown of long, sharp thorns and put it on his head, and they put a royal purple robe on him. "Hail! King of the Jews!" they mocked, and they hit him with their fists.

JESUS IS CONDEMNED TO DEATH

LUKE 23:23-26

The crowd shouted louder and louder for Jesus' death, and their voices prevailed. So Pilate sentenced Jesus to die as they demanded. As they had requested, he released Barabbas, the man in prison for insurrection and murder. But he delivered Jesus over to them to do as they wished.

As they led Jesus away, Simon of Cyrene, who was coming in from the country just then, was forced to follow Jesus and carry his cross.

JESUS IS NAILED TO A CROSS

LUKE 23:32-34

Two others, both criminals, were led out to be executed with him. Finally, they came to a place called The Skull. All three were crucified there – Jesus on the center cross, and the two criminals on either side.

Jesus said, "Father, forgive these people, because they don't know what they are doing."

And the soldiers gambled for his clothes by throwing dice.

JESUS AND HIS MOTHER

JOHN 19:25-27

Standing near the cross were Jesus' mother, and his mother's sister, Mary (the wife of Clopas), and Mary Magdalene. When Jesus saw his mother standing there beside the disciple he loved, he said to her, "Woman, he is your son." And he said to this disciple, "She is your mother."

And from then on this disciple took her into his home.

JESUS GIVES HIS LIFE FOR US

LUKE 23:44-48

By this time it was noon, and darkness fell across the whole land until three o'clock. The light from the sun was gone. And suddenly, the thick veil hanging in the Temple was torn apart. Then Jesus shouted, "Father, I entrust my spirit into your hands!" And with those words he breathed his last.

When the captain of the Roman soldiers handling the executions saw what had happened, he praised God and said, "Surely this man was innocent."

And when the crowd that came to see the crucifixion saw all that had happened, they went home in deep sorrow.

JESUS IS PUT IN A TOMB

LUKE 23:50, 52-53, 55-56

Now there was a good and righteous man named Joseph.

He went to Pilate and asked for Jesus' body. Then he took the body down from the cross and wrapped it in a long linen cloth and laid it in a new tomb that had been carved out of rock.

The women from Galilee followed and saw the tomb where they placed his body. Then they went home and prepared spices and ointments to embalm him.

But by the time they were finished it was the Sabbath, so they rested all that day as required by the law.

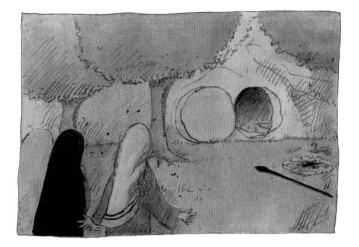

THE TOMB IS EMPTY

JOHN 20:1-10

Early Sunday morning, while it was still dark, Mary Magdalene came to the tomb and found that the stone had been rolled away from the entrance. She ran and found Simon Peter and the other disciple, the one whom Jesus loved.

She said, "They have taken the Lord's body out of the tomb, and I don't know where they have put him!"

Peter and the other disciple ran to the tomb to see. The other disciple outran Peter and got there first. He stooped and looked in and saw the linen cloth lying there, but he didn't go in.

Then Simon Peter arrived and went inside. He also noticed the linen wrappings lying there, while the cloth that had covered Jesus' head was folded up and lying to the side. Then the other disciple also went in, and he saw and believed – for until then they hadn't realized that the Scriptures said he would rise from the dead.

Then they went home.

JESUS IS RAISED FROM DEATH

MARK 16:9-13

It was early on Sunday morning when Jesus rose from the dead, and the first person who saw him was Mary Magdalene, the woman from whom he had cast out seven demons. She went and found the disciples, who were grieving and weeping. But when she told them that Jesus was alive and she had seen him, they didn't believe her.

Afterward he appeared to two who were walking from Jerusalem into the country, but they didn't recognize him at first because he had changed his appearance. When they realized who he was, they rushed back to tell the others, but no one believed them.

JESUS APPEARS TO HIS DISCIPLES

JOHN 20:19-29; 21:1-14

That evening, on the first day of the week, the disciples were meeting behind locked doors because they were afraid of the Jewish leaders. Suddenly, Jesus was standing there among them! "Peace be with you," he said. As he spoke, he held out his hands for them to see, and he showed them his side. They were filled with joy when they saw their Lord!

He spoke to them again and said, "Peace be with you. As the Father has sent me, so I send you." Then he breathed on them and said to them, "Receive the Holy Spirit. If you forgive anyone's sins, they are forgiven. If you refuse to forgive them, they are unforgiven."

One of the disciples, Thomas (nicknamed the Twin), was not with the others when Jesus came. They told him, "We have seen the Lord!"

But he replied, "I won't believe it unless I see the nail wounds in his hands, put my fingers into them, and place my hand into the wound in his side."

Eight days later the disciples were together again, and this time Thomas was with them. The doors were locked; but suddenly, as before, Jesus was standing among them. He said, "Peace be with you." Then he said to Thomas, "Put your finger here and see my hands. Put your hand into the wound in my side. Don't be faithless any longer. Believe!"

"My Lord and my God!" Thomas exclaimed.

Then Jesus told him, "You believe because you have seen me. Blessed are those who haven't seen me and believe anyway."

Later Jesus appeared again to the disciples beside the Sea of Galilee. This is how it happened. Several of the disciples were there – Simon Peter, Thomas (nicknamed the Twin), Nathanael from Cana in Galilee, the sons of Zebedee, and two other disciples.

Simon Peter said, "I'm going fishing."

"We'll come, too," they all said. So they went out in the boat, but they caught nothing all night.

At dawn the disciples saw Jesus standing on the beach, but they couldn't see who he was. He called out, "Friends, have you caught any fish?"

"No," they replied.

Then he said, "Throw out your net on the right-hand side of the boat, and you'll get plenty of fish!"

So they did, and they couldn't draw in the net because there were so many fish in it.

Then the disciple whom Jesus loved said to Peter, "It is the Lord!"

When Simon Peter heard that it was the Lord, he put on his tunic (for he had stripped for work), jumped into the water, and swam ashore. The others stayed with the boat and pulled the loaded net to the shore, for they were only out about three hundred feet.

When they got there, they saw that a charcoal fire was burning and fish were frying over it, and there was bread.

"Bring some of the fish you've just caught," Jesus said.

So Simon Peter went aboard and dragged the net to the shore. There were one hundred and fifty-three large fish, and yet the net hadn't torn.

"Now come and have some breakfast!" Jesus said.

And no one dared ask him if he really was the Lord because they were sure of it. Then Jesus served them the bread and the fish

This was the third time Jesus had appeared to his disciples since he had been raised from the dead.

JESUS SENDS HIS FOLLOWERS OUT TO PREACH

MATTHEW 28:16-20

Then the eleven disciples left for Galilee, going to the mountain where Jesus had told them to go. When they saw him, they worshiped him – but some of them still doubted!

Jesus came and told his disciples, "I have been given complete authority in heaven and on earth. Therefore, go and make disciples of all the nations, baptizing them in the name of the Father and the Son and the Holy Spirit. Teach these new disciples to obey all the commands I have given you. And be sure of this: I am with you always, even to the end of the age."

JESUS GOES BACK TO HIS FATHER

LUKE 24:50; ACTS 1:8-11

Then Jesus led them to Bethany, and lifting his hands to heaven, he blessed them. "But when the Holy Spirit has come upon you, you will receive power and will tell people about me everywhere – in Jerusalem, throughout Judea, in Samaria, and to the ends of the earth."

It was not long after he said this that he was taken up into the sky while they were watching, . . .

205

. . . and he disappeared into a cloud.

As they were straining their eyes to see him, two white-robed men suddenly stood there among them. They said, "Men of Galilee, why are you standing here staring at the sky? Jesus has been taken away from you into heaven. And someday, just as you saw him go, he will return!"

PART SIX

JESUS IS ALWAYS WITH US

JESUS SENDS THE HOLY SPIRIT

ACTS 1:12-14; 2:1-8

The apostles were at the Mount of Olives when this happened, so they walked the half mile back to Jerusalem. Then they went to the upstairs room of the house where they were staying. Here is the list of those who were present: Peter, John, James, Andrew, Philip, Thomas, Bartholomew, Matthew, James (son of Alphaeus), Simon (the Zealot), and Judas (son of James).

They all met together continually for prayer, along with Mary the mother of Jesus, several other women, and the brothers of Jesus.

On the day of Pentecost, seven weeks after Jesus' resurrection, the believers were meeting together in one place. Suddenly, there was a sound from heaven like the roaring of a mighty windstorm in the skies above them, and it filled the house where they were meeting. Then, what looked like flames or tongues of fire appeared and settled on each of them.

And everyone present was filled with the Holy Spirit and began speaking in other languages, as the Holy Spirit gave them this ability.

Godly Jews from many nations were living in Jerusalem at that time. When they heard this sound, they came running to see what it was all about, and they were bewildered to hear their own languages being spoken by the believers. They were beside themselves with wonder. "How can this be?" they exclaimed. "These people are all from Galilee, and yet we hear them speaking the languages of the lands where we were born!

THE FOLLOWERS AFTER PENTECOST

ACTS 4:32-33; 5:14

All the believers were of one heart and mind, and they felt that what they owned was not their own; they shared everything they had.

And the apostles gave powerful witness to the resurrection of the Lord Jesus, and God's great favor was upon them all.

And more and more people believed and were brought to the Lord – crowds of both men and women.

PREACHING THE GOSPEL

This good news of the risen Jesus was told by Peter, Paul, and the apostles; then by those who came after them, the bishops. The story of Jesus was written down by Matthew, Mark, Luke, and John in the four Gospels. It was passed on for two thousand years by the Church, that is, by all those who have been baptized.

BAPTISM

Before he went back to his Father, the risen Jesus said to his followers: "Therefore, go and make disciples of all the nations, baptizing them in the name of the Father and the Son and the Holy Spirit. Teach these new disciples to obey all the commands I have given you. And be sure of this: I am with you always, even to the end of the age." (MATTHEW 28:19-20)

Through baptism we become the beloved children of God and the followers of Jesus. Jesus himself asked to be baptized. He made his Father happy, and he calls us to make his Father happy, too. He is always with us.

213

But how is Jesus always with us?
How can we be his disciples?

Our daily life

Jesus said, "Your love for one another will prove to the world that you are my disciples." (*JOHN 13:35*)
So every day when we love those who are around us, Jesus is with us.

In our work

By doing our work as well as we can, we love our neighbor, too. And Jesus is with us.

INVENTIONS AND CREATIONS

By using our gifts and our intelligence to create and invent everything that is beautiful and good for people and for the earth, we share in God's creation. So Jesus is with us.

HELPING EACH OTHER

Jesus said, "When you did it to one of the least of these my brothers and sisters, you were doing it to me!" (*MATTHEW 25:40*)
So when we help those who suffer, Jesus is with us.

PRAYING

When we think about God and his word, Jesus is with us. And he is with us when we thank him, and when we ask him to help us not to give up. When we long for him to forgive us, and when we trust him in the way a little child trusts, then Jesus is among us.

That can happen wherever we are. But Jesus also likes it when we take time to stop and, on our own or together with others, say the prayer he himself taught us to pray: the Lord's Prayer, Our Father.

THE EUCHARIST

Jesus said, "I am the living bread that came down out of heaven. . . . All who eat my flesh and drink my blood remain in me, and I in them." (JOHN 6:51, 56).

Jesus knows how weak we are, so he wants to give himself to us to teach us about his love for us and to help us to do all the good things he wants us to do. When we share in the Eucharist (also called the Lord's Supper, or Holy Communion, or Mass), Jesus is with us, closer than ever.

220

THE HOLY SPIRIT

Jesus said, "But when the Father sends the Counselor as my representative – and by the Counselor I mean the Holy Spirit – he will teach you everything and will remind you of everything I myself have told you." (*JOHN 14:26*)

When we long for the Holy Spirit, when we ask to be confirmed, and when we pray for the Holy Spirit's help, the Holy Spirit does help us. He helps us to understand the Bible, and he gives us the strength to tell others about God's love. The Holy Spirit is God's great gift. He is the Spirit of Jesus, always with us.

FORGIVENESS RECEIVED

Jesus said, "Heaven will be happier over one lost sinner who returns to God than over ninety-nine others who are righteous and haven't strayed away!" (LUKE 15:7)

Even if we stop thinking about Jesus and stop loving him, he never leaves us. He is like a shepherd who goes out hunting for his lost sheep. When we go back to him, God is very happy, like the father of the son who left home.

When Jesus had been raised from death, he said to his followers:

"Receive the Holy Spirit. If you forgive anyone's sins, they are forgiven." (JOHN 20:22, 23)

That is why, when the priest tells us we are forgiven, we know we really are forgiven.

FORGIVENESS GIVEN

Jesus said, "If you forgive those who sin against you, your heavenly Father will forgive you." *(MATTHEW 6:14)*
So when we forgive each other, Jesus is with us.

TOGETHER

Jesus said, "Where two or three gather together because they are mine, I am there among them." (*MATTHEW 18:20*)
So when we meet together in his name, as followers of Jesus and for him, Jesus is among us.

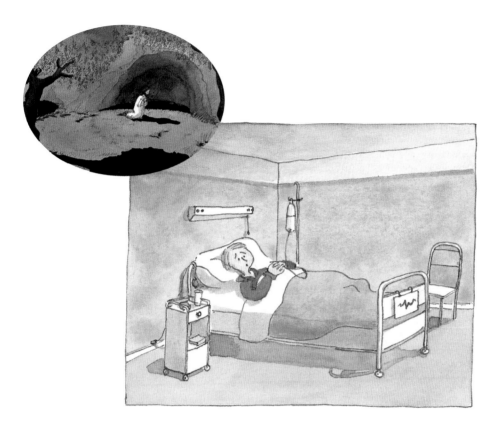

SUFFERING

At the Mount of Olives, Jesus said to his Father: "Father, if you are willing, please take this cup of suffering away from me. Yet I want your will, not mine." (*LUKE 22:42*)

Sometimes we may have to go through suffering. Sometimes, out of love for people around us, we may have to do difficult things and we may be afraid. At times like these we must pray in the way Jesus prayed. And he will always be with us to help us.

MARY

When he was on the cross, Jesus said to Mary and John: "Woman, he is your son," and, "She is your mother." *(JOHN 19:26, 27)*

John was the only one of Jesus' disciples who was at the foot of the cross. He stands for each of us. Jesus gave Mary to John, to be John's mother. In the same way, Jesus gives Mary to each one of us, to be a mother to us. With Mary, we will be better able to understand Jesus' love for us, and we will be willing to stay with him, just like John.

WEDDINGS

Jesus said, "A man leaves his father and mother and is joined to his wife, and the two are united into one.' Since they are no longer two but one, let no one separate them, for God has joined them together." *(MATTHEW 19:5-6)*

When a man and woman get married before God, promising to love each other forever, and welcome children, Jesus blesses them. As long as they stay with Jesus, their love will never stop growing.

DEVOTED LIVES

Jesus said, "Everyone who has given up houses or brothers or sisters or father or mother or children or property, for my sake, will receive a hundred times as much in return and will have eternal life." (MATTHEW 19:29)

Jesus is close to those who answer his call – people like priests, nuns, monks, and those who give up all they have to preach his gospel. They never stop praying. They never stop caring for sick and poor people.

THE SAINTS

Jesus said, "When you obey me, you remain in my love, just as I obey my Father and remain in his love. I have told you this so that you will be filled with my joy. Yes, your joy will overflow!" (*JOHN 15:10-11*)

The saints understand that they have received everything from God. They love Jesus. They listen to his word and never stop asking him to help them to do what he wants. Jesus gives them the strength of the Holy Spirit and shares his joy with them.

St. Peter, St. Paul, the holy Apostles, and many others were killed because they were followers of Jesus. They were helped by the strength and joy of the Holy Spirit.

Throughout the centuries, there have been many saints. In the fifth century, St. Patrick set off to preach the gospel in Ireland. He went because Jesus had said: "Go and make disciples of all the nations." (MATTHEW 28:19)

In the eighth century, St. Boniface set out as well, risking his own life. He was "the apostle of Germany."

In the twelfth century, St. Francis of Assisi lived by Jesus' words: "God blesses those whose hearts are pure, for they will see God." (MATTHEW 5:8)

St. Francis chose to be poor in order to be rich with God.

In the sixteenth century, St. Thomas More showed the purity of his heart by his obedience to God. God came first in his life. He died on the scaffold.

In the sixteenth century, St. John of God fully understood Jesus' words:
"When you did it to one of the least of these my brothers and sisters, you were doing it to me!" (*MATTHEW 25:40*)
He stood up for all those who were ill or had nothing at all.

Again in the sixteenth century, St. Teresa of Avila realized one day that to please God she must rely on his strength and not on her own. Jesus said: "Those who remain in me, and I in them, will produce much fruit. For apart from me you can do nothing." (JOHN 15:5)

From then on, St. Teresa kept on praying to God, and she started many monasteries.

In the seventeenth century, St. Vincent de Paul was very upset by the poverty all around him. So he helped the poor and ill people and children who had no homes and no family of their own. He showed great love.

In the nineteenth century, St. Teresa of Lisieux understood that to be a saint, there is no need to carry out great deeds, but to do any deed, even the smallest ones, with love for Jesus.

In the twentieth century, St. Maximilien Kolbe was touched by Jesus' words to John: "She is your mother." (JOHN 19:27)

After that, St. Maximilien endlessly did everything to have Mary honored, and he gave up his life to save a man.

Only a few years ago, Mother Teresa died. She loved and took care of the poorest among the poor people. She found that each poor person represented Jesus, who was "thirsty" to be loved.

There have been, and there still are, many saints throughout all the world. Some are well known and some are not so well known. Just as he invited them, so Jesus invites each one of us to keep on asking him for his Holy Spirit, for strength to do what Jesus wants us to do, and for his joy. Jesus wants to share his joy with us. As we wait for Jesus to come again, we know that his words are true: "Be sure of this: I am with you always, even to the end of the age." (*MATTHEW 28:20*)